TRANSIENT VISITORS

Month 1, A Collection of Very Tiny Tales

DAVID O'BOYLE

Contents

For my first brother, who taught me to question.

For my second brother, who taught me to answer.

Preface

Rule 1. Keep it short. Rule 2. Entertain. My guiding principles for writing *Transient Visitors: Month 1 of 12, a Collection of Very Tiny Tales.* Within those constraints, I let my imagine wonder. These stories are the end result of whatever it brought back.

"Fathers and Sons", Fathers and Sons

"Who needs tickets? Who wants tickets?"

During the reign of the old Yankee Stadium, that type of sales pitch screamed scam to native New Yorkers. However, to out-of-towners, it was chum in the water. They took the bait like sharks in a frenzy. Then scalpers hooked their money.

When the new stadium replaced the old one, such grifting went the way of the dinosaurs. Scalping became lawful commerce carried out by former hustlers turned quasi-customer service agents. Last season, they'd take your money and run. This year, they'd basically put on a bearskin hat and escort you to the turnstile for your tickets in clear, queen's royal guard style.

"This place has lost its grit," my dad grumbled.

It wouldn't be a day out unless he complained about the younger generation of snowflakes snipping away at the fabric of American society. Making matters worse, we were standing in line waiting to scan our phone tickets. So, not only was he contending with snowflakes, he was up against technology, his ultimate foe.

I did my best to ignore him and not let his words take away from the spectacle before us. The golden granite and limestone hall of the New Yankee Stadium is a sport's Sistine chapel. Yet while it is majestic; while it is a shrine to the American pastime; and while it is an architectural achievement; it's not the House that Ruth built. And it never would be. The House that Ruth Built was created by divine baseball bat. The new place was created by men with trowels and tractors.

"I liked the old one better," my dad said, annoyingly echoing my own thoughts. While I appreciated his honesty, I wished he kept those thoughts to himself. That is, unless he wanted to pay for his own last-minute ticket to a Yankees/Red Sox game.

But he had a point. I would have liked my kids to experience the Bronx in the glory days rather than now, especially with the rivals in town; I would have liked them to walk in from exit 4 or 5 on the Major Deegan and see the old jailhouse, a multi-floored building boxed in by barbed wire and barred windows; I would have liked them to hear the borough's best jazz— the percussive pandemonium the inmates played from inside their cages after a Yankee win. I was their age the first time I heard it. Coming full circle, it also was a Yankee/Red Sox game. From that day forward, I'd known the transcendent power of this organization. Even when justice wouldn't serve man, there were the Yankees.

Yet now the jail was gone. A soulless Target stood in its place. In the land of the incarcerated, I couldn't imagine a worse feeling than leaving a jailhouse overlooking Yankee stadium for a river view at Rikers.

A stroll through monument park when we got inside the

stadium revived my positive energy. In fact, by the time we reached our left field seats, I didn't even care to complain about the price of beer; or foam fingers; or jerseys; or more curly fries for the kids. Whatever anyone wanted, they got, within reason.

The baseball gods seemed to be rewarding my generosity. By the seventh inning stretch, the game was still close. As much as I like to drub the sox, I make an exception to that rule while in physical attendance. Nobody wants a blowout at the ball-park. When that happens, you feel gipped. Instead, you want what we had, a game where a knot forms in your stomach when a runner gets on first and the best hitter on the field is clicking his cleats in the batter's box.

The pitcher snapped a curve over for strike one.

The batter belted strike two into the left field grandstand. A struggle in the row behind me ensued, which climaxed when the ball rolled down, right underneath my feet, right where both of my boys could pounce.

I don't know how, but while they were down there, both boys had an equal hold on the ball. Before long, the scene became a spectacle—first in the section; then on the jumbotron; then on the YES network; and then on Sports-Center and YouTube and CNN.

What did that mean? It meant that in one way or another, the world bore witness to my next parenting move. Worse than the world, my wife, the biggest Yankee fan in the family, was too. Damn work from home. She never missed a game since going remote. You try to do something nice, you know? And what happens? You end up stuck in a predicament worthy of Solomon without any of his wisdom.

Thankfully my dad had some.

He yanked the ball from both of his grandson's hands and chucked it back onto the field.

"Sorry, boys. Red Sox home run. Had to toss it back," he said.

The crowd, including my two boys, cheered wildly in support of dad/grandpa's dedicated fandom.

I did the same, for that reason and more.

2

Own Medicine

Harold Morton Meade took off his chukkas and sat Indian style on his chair. Once his legs were folded, he propped his keyboard on his monitor and greased down his desk with a pocket wipe.

Guillermo watched Harold's routine from his office security monitor. If nodding off after a mid-morning coffee break was a one-time thing, Guillermo would have overlooked it. New to the company and his managerial role, he was wary of beginning his reign with an iron-fist. It could cause dissent among the ranks, even if the first head to roll fell from the body of a lazy slug like Harold.

Still, Guillermo had a job to do. Part of that job demanded a certain quality work product. If Harold did respectable work and treated himself to an occasional snooze, that was one thing. It was another thing entirely to hand in crap so he could keep on sleeping. That process gave Guillermo two jobs to do—his own and Harold's— and it was killing him.

Days at the office therefore spilled into nights. Arrivals earlier. Departures later.

Guillermo rubbed his eyes. Then he looked around his office. Old coffee mugs stacked high around his desk like skyscrapers, obstructing his views.

This had to stop. It was time for the slug to get salted.

Guillermo hit the intercom to contact his personal assistant. "Laura Lynn, please set up a meeting for me and Harold in the conference room today."

"What time?" Laura Lynn asked.

"After lunch. Let him have a last meal," Guillermo said.

Laura Lynn set the meeting for 3:45 pm. Harold came inside the conference room at 4:10 pm. As he sat down opposite Guillermo and Laura Lynn, he apologized for the delay. 'An urgent matter had to be finished,' he said, and his computer 'wasn't cooperating.' Guillermo wondered if the urgent matter was a dream and his computer complications came from using his keyboard for a pillow.

"Coffee?" Laura Lynn asked.

"I've had more than enough today, Laura Lynn, thank you," Guillermo said.

"Same here," Harold said.

The consummate professionals, Guillermo and Laura Lynn refrained from informing Harold that the caffeine wasn't working.

With the coffee situation resolved, Laura Lynn left the conference room. When she was on the other side of the door, she smiled at Guillermo through an adjacent window and gave him a nod of encouragement. *First firings. Never an easy thing,* she thought.

Since he knew that Harold moonlighted at one of the local oyster bars, Guillermo inquired about the seafood festival next month. The question certainly calmed tensions, but it redirected the conversation too far from Guillermo's goal. As his boss, he should have known better. When Harold Morton Meade had the chance to talk about anything other than work, the slug turned into a salesman.

A half-hour passed without progress. Then, when Guillermo thought all hope lost, Harold tripped on his own snare. During his tired explanation on oyster preparation, Harold paused twice to warn Guillermo about 'purchase-to-shucking-time.'

"You need to purchase the oysters and shuck them as soon as possible," Harold said. "Let them sit too long, and they'll suffer. When they suffer, so does your gut."

"That reminds me of why I called this meeting, Harold," Guillermo said.

The manager stumbled through the preamble of his five-minute firing speech. By minute two of the speech, Guillermo's eyes got heavy. By minute three, they closed. By minute four, Harold was the only person awake in the conference room.

Laura Lynn looked at the clock on her computer screen. The five-minute meeting with Harold had just passed the one-hour mark. What was taking so long? She headed to the conference room to see if Guillermo needed any help.

It turned out what he really needed, what both men really needed, were blankets.

Both Harold Morton Meade and Guillermo were sound asleep on opposite sides of the conference room table.

3

Raid of the Zombie-Mummies II

C lemens looked at the DVD in his hand. *Finally*, he thought, finally he'd convinced Ivo to watch *Raid of the Zombie-Mummies II*. They'd seen the original together last summer. That debacle had convinced Clemens his best friend was done with the genre. What a difference a year can make.

Still, old habits die hard. As soon as Ivo conceded to watching *Raid of the Zombie Mummies II,* Clemens had to test his nerve.

He did so when the film climaxed. In the movie scene, a zombie-mummy lay in wait behind the door of a child's upstairs bedroom. Right as the child ran frantic into his room to escape pursuers on the main floor, the zombie-mummy popped out. When this happened, Clemens grabbed Ivo's shoulder and screamed. Equal parts embarrassed by his terrified reaction and annoyed at Clemens for causing it, Ivo told him to leave. Unlike countless other weekend nights, Clemens would not be crashing on the couch. Sleep would have to wait until he finished the long walk home.

Besides the occasional moonbeam reflecting off the barbed wire fence, one side of Eustis Street was pitch black. Only locals like Clemens knew what the fence surrounded: a small airport for aviation hobbyists. Only locals like Clemens also knew where to find the holes in the fence. Committing them to memory was key for quicker treks across town.

The other side of Eustis Street was also blanketed in blackness, but it was a suburban blackness, not an abysmal one, meaning it received some illumination from spotty streetlights, and the occasional flashing television. Cartoon Network played on one particularly massive plasma screen on the second floor of a nearby house.

This caught Clemens's attention.

It caught something else's too.

That something was thin, maybe twelve feet tall. When it stretched its torso out like an accordion, it doubled in size, making it tall enough to lean against the balcony above the portico and watch the show flat-footed from the ground. Considering the clarity of the screen from Clemens's spot on the street, it didn't seem like the thing needed a better view. But apparently that's what it wanted. Efforts to scale the balcony above the portico began with hoisting the left side of its body up and over the balustrade. This went easy enough. Attempts to do the same with the right side of its body were less effective. Five unsuccessful tries later, it dismounted back onto the front lawn with both feet.

Which is when their eyes met.

From its first lunge toward him, Clemens knew he couldn't outrun it. Sliding through the next opening in the old airport fence and finding cover was his only option.

Forty-five minutes and many mosquito bites later, Clemens lifted the evergreen hedge off his head and deemed the coast clear. Despite dropping *Revenge of the Zombie Mummies II* during the scramble, he declared his retreat a victory. Finding the DVD could wait until tomorrow. Tonight, he'd have to focus on apologizing to Ivo. Present circumstances made the long journey home up Eustis Street, or back down for that matter, too dangerous.

Better to get off the street. Better to navigate through the airport. Clemens knew if he stayed due north, he'd eventually reach the airport administrative cabin. Ivo's house was just east of there.

All went according to plan until Clemens reached the airport administrative cabin and turned toward his friend's house. From his new eastern vantage point, he noticed a light on in the administrative cabin that was earlier obscured from view.

Someone was inside.

No, some*thing* was inside.

His something. All twelve feet of it. Curled up in a rocking chair. Watching television.

This time though, the images on the screen were not animated. Perhaps its developing taste demanded a drama. Clemens moved in for a closer look. When he did, he saw a kid on the screen running upstairs away from a band of zombie-mummies on the main floor. Horror, then, not drama. Clemens's type of horror.

So, the thing had taken his DVD. And by its body language, it was pretty scared of its contents. Maybe even more scared than Ivo.

Clemens couldn't resist. Right as the kid on screen closed the door, revealing the zombie-mummy waiting behind it, Clemens banged on the window and screamed. Then he ran back to Ivo's house, unsure of whether he was fueled by laughter, or terror, or both.

What he was sure of, however, was that nothing in that old airport had ever been as terrified as that thing, whatever it was.

4

Furlough

Two and a half hours and two cups of coffee.

That's how Marc Pontruff answered the question, 'how long does it take to get to Wyatt, New Jersey.'

Ten years ago, his response would sound less staged. Back then, Ma was still around and Pop had a little juice left in his knees, not to mention a functional memory. Under those circumstances, he could justify sporadic visits. Not anymore. Not after Pop turned ninety last winter and needed near-constant care. The situation left Marc Pontruff with two choices. He could either take long drives to Wyatt or short drives to a nursing home. He chose the former.

"It's more and more errands every day. He won't even walk down the driveway to get the mail anymore. If it wasn't for me, I'm not sure his neighbors would know he still lived there," Marc told Lita in between toothbrush strokes.

"You really have to go again tomorrow?" his wife asked without lifting her eyes from her book titled, *Management in the Digital Age*.

Marc Pontruff nodded as he crawled into bed, conscious of where his comments ranked on his wife's list of priorities. "Gotta pick up some of his prescriptions tomorrow morning, then I'm going back to Wyatt. Wanna join?"

"You know I can't take off," Lita said without pause. "Big day tomorrow."

Mark knew better than to question her about anything work-related. As much as he wanted to say she was being crazy; that she deserved to take one of her many personal days accrued over a decade of company service, he kept quiet. When he noticed the chapter she was reading from *Management in the Digital Age*, titled "On Millennials," he was thankful he did. Fifty-something Lita worked for a business swarming with young professionals. Given her tendency to snap at age-related issues, he steered the conversation away from that minefield.

"I'll be gone before you wake up," Marc said as he kissed her goodnight and shut the light on his side of the bed.

THE LIGHT ON LITA'S SIDE DID JUST THE OPPOSITE. IT BURNED deep into the night, illuminating her preparation for her "big day tomorrow." This consisted of a one-on-one meeting with Morlin, the founder and CEO of her company. Experience with Morlin and his history of terminating unproductive staff made her prep for the worst. If her head was bound for the chopping block, he'd have to hear her quote *Management in the Digital Age*, his own book, while her head rolled.

Per usual, the meeting was not the doomsday scenario Lita anticipated. Yes, Morlin had some constructive criticism, which, for someone like Lita, was hard to swallow. But it was only a side dish of the meeting. He also spooned out heaps of praise and a promotion.

"Under one condition," Morlin said. "You take the rest of the day for yourself. Accrued time off is there to use. It's unfashionable as a badge of honor."

Energized and excited by her promotion, Lita wanted to call Mark and relay the good news. Then a better idea surfaced. Mark loved a good surprise. He also liked booze and beef. With those two things in mind, Lita grabbed some steaks from the butcher and some wine from the liquor store. Then she headed to Pop's house for dinner, confident that Marc would be happy as a gull to get some food, and appreciative of her efforts to see Pop for the first time in almost a year—since the last holiday season.

When she pulled up to the house in Wyatt, it looked like more than a year had passed. Lita hardly recognized the place with all the improvements. But for the GPS announcing her arrival, she would've driven right by. *Odd that Marc didn't mention these changes*, she thought to herself. Such lack of communication bothered her. How things used to be, Lita would have heard about every screw that hit the drywall during the renovation.

This had to change. Armed with dinner and a bottle of red, there was no better time to start then now.

She entered Pop's house how she used to enter her own home—with a youthful magnetism that demanded a bedroom hello from her husband, who in those days waited for her at the door like an excited little puppy. Would time repeat itself tonight?

Not exactly. Marc Pontruff was not waiting at the door like a little puppy. He was napping on the couch with a beer between his briefs and a bag of chips on his belly, like an old dog.

"Where's Pop?" Lita asked as she kissed his forehead and

put the wine on the coffee table. Marc's initial reaction was puzzling. True, she could understand him being startled. But he looked more than startled. He looked guilty. Lita soon learned why.

Pop had been dead since January.

5

Sniffers

Smoke rose from Chastity's cigarette. As the flame climbed toward the tipping paper, she wondered whether the particulates it dispensed into the air were dirtier than the potential patrons stumbling by. She didn't think so. Maybe that's why she bought cigarettes and the drunks stumbling by bought her.

It took half of breaktime to find the right target. When he finally appeared, Wolfy, the bouncer standing in front of the red roping, saw him too. Wolfy had worked the door at Stephania's long enough to ID a sucker almost as fast as the strippers.

"How much do you think you'll get from him?" Wolfy asked.

"Ten times cover," Chastity said, adjusting her footwear.

"Sounds about right," Wolfy said. "Lemme get him over here."

The bouncer yelled terms across the street. Their prey, who at the moment was playing air guitar under the main window of a live music bar, declined the invitation.

"Disregard the sign. No cover," Wolfy said.

The hook was set. In a minute, the air guitarist left his sidewalk stage and entered Stephania's. Chastity's hand stroked his back before his feet left the welcome mat.

"Hey, Hun. Sit down with me over there?" she said, directing him to two chairs in the back. When they settled into the new spot and started talking, Chastity confirmed her customer did not frequent strip clubs.

"Happy to hear it," Chastity said with a seductive smile. Her statement was true. But not for the reasons implied. Chastity was happy to hear it because nice folks in strip clubs dole out coin like kids at a wishing well. They slip you tips just for normal, clothes-on conversation.

"Chastity to the stage," the emcee said over the loudspeaker.

"That's me," she said.

"How can I get you to stay?" he said as she rose from her chair.

"Pay for a dance. Then they'll skip my turn," she said.

"Fine. Let's do it. Let's have a dance," he said, struggling to come to terms with what he was negotiating. Problem was, you stay too long at a wishing well, you want to get wet. That's when the trouble starts.

Chastity grabbed him by the hand and led him to a back room. After helping her patron to a comfortable seat on the couch, she mounted his crotch and began to move with the rhythm of the song. During the refrain, she reversed her body so her backside faced his front. He gave her a nudge to wedge her closer between his legs. She let it slide because his demand was gentle. During a dance, clients did far worse to Chastity for far less.

Then she felt it. A cold, wet, set of nostrils slimed up her spine. It wasn't the act itself that frightened her. It was knowing the source of the sound, and that it emitted from a Sniffer, nature's most powerful nose.

Chastity tried to run. Cold steel ratcheted around her wrists before she reached the door.

"Wolfy!" she screamed.

The bouncer came running, ready to make one of his customary rescues. Once he saw the patron's nose, he changed course. A nose only swells to such a massive size if it belongs to a Sniffer; and everyone knows you don't get in the way of a Sniffer. They only look for one thing: intergalactic fugitives in disguise.

As the Sniffer read Chastity her rights, Wolfy wondered a few things. First, what did the little stripper do to attract such specific law enforcement expertise. For you only needed a Sniffer if a suspect had undergone the most extreme black-market changeling surgery, whereby all that was left of their former selves was the slightest trace of genetic code, undetectable to all but a Sniffer.

Second, who was she, really?

The bouncer remembered something, shuddered, and prayed he didn't know the answer to both questions.

6

Bound for the Baptism

Bruno bent down one of the horizontal slats with his finger, permitting a few rays of Texas sun to enter his dorm room. Temporary blindness was a relief, a shield from his worries beyond the window, the biggest one being what waited for him in the river behind campus. Such relief was short lived, however. A puffy cumulous cloud soon swallowed the sun, returning all freshmen heading down to the river back into view. All of them, Bruno too, were bound for the Baptism, a freshman rite of passage on day one of fall semester. Everyone new to campus climbed the sacred tree, swung on the sacred swing, and splashed into the sacred river.

Sure, it sounded fun, breaking the ice with the other newbies while waiting to receive the sacrament. Every guy wanted to talk football, smoke weed, and chug cheap liquor. The girls sunbathing on the river rocks did too.

But for Bruno, this 'fun' was a nightmare. Traditions like these ate up fat kids who couldn't swim. Howard, another portly freshman he met down by the water, was proof of that.

Unwilling to take off his shirt or swing into the river, Howard was already persona non grata—the resident outcast, the betrayer of tradition. Bruno was Howard all through high school. He would not be Howard in college.

Bring on the river.

A familiar face from his dorm floor, Sam was his name, was handling the rope for everyone. Sam sat on the horizontal branch above the river where the rope was tied. After someone swung into the river, he caught the recoil and brought it to the next person in line. In exchange for his labors, he could skip the line and jump whenever he pleased.

Nobody minded. When Sam swung, each twist and turn was a separate stanza to his poetry in motion. The show was meant for brighter lights than sun rays reflecting on the river.

"Bruno, right?" Sam asked when Bruno reached the front of the line. "Nice to meet you. I think we're in the same dorm."

Bruno stayed quiet. Sam sensed his silence as fear rather than rudeness and responded accordingly. "It's no big deal, man. The scariest thing about it is thinking you jumped in with your phone," Sam said.

Bruno laughed. "That's why I kept it charging back in my room. Hang on to my wallet for a bit?"

"Sure thing," Sam said as he took the wallet and handed Bruno the rope.

"I'm here. I won't let anything happen to you," Sam whispered in response to seeing his dormmate's two trembling hands.

Bruno knew Sam was someone he could trust. So, he gripped the rope tight and swung out onto the river.

Panic set in as soon as he splashed into the water. Sam jumped in the second he started screaming and pulled him to shore.

Already anticipating Bruno's humiliation, Sam said, "Psyche!" to all the worried freshman crowding the bank. Bruno went with it, the continued look of panic on his face fast appearing like performance. A few folks considered fake drowning a non-laughing matter. Most found it hysterical. At least for now, the freshman class found their campus comedians.

"Thanks for saving my ass out there," Bruno said when he and Sam had a moment alone.

"No problem. You got me next time," Sam said.

"If there is a next time," Bruno said.

"There's always a next time in college," Sam said.

Bruno smiled and asked for his wallet.

Sam's smile changed to a look of alarm. The wallet was gone, likely lost to the bottom of the river during all the commotion.

"I can pay you back," Sam said.

But it wasn't about money. Bruno's wallet contained his fake ID. When it disappeared, so did his nightlife, a fact that became all too real when he departed one way from the river—to the dorm— and everyone else went the other—toward the bars on main. Yet rather than mope, Bruno appreciated the positives. For one, him and Sam seemed friendship-bound. That would never have happened in high school. To have it happen on the first day of college was worth ten fake IDs. For two, his current isolation was a bit overblown. He still had his phone. And Sam kept him updated.

Up until the last text message that correspondence was going great. Then Sam sent him a snapchat of a fat kid grinding between two beautiful girls.

Howard.

7

The Skater

The ice crunching under our skates sounded the dinner bell for the Zamboni. It also notified the teenagers wearing yellow 'Parks Department Staff' shirts to round us up. Time to switch rinks.

Normally we wouldn't tolerate the delay involved in this migration process. But it was the first snow of the season, so even the Parks Department got a pass. Twenty-four hours from now they wouldn't be so lucky. Moods change. Winter wonderlands go from relieving tension to creating it. Today's snow is tomorrow's slush.

Not tolerating delay also requires the energy to complain. We didn't have that. Any anger or willingness to do so was outweighed by exhaustion. With so many people chewing up the ice at once, we were essentially skating on snow. The extra effort involved made people glad to rest, and generally more inclined to conserve their breath than to waste it yelling at staff suffering from cystic acne.

But having your lungs and your skating legs ready for the next rink only addressed physical preparation. To enjoy yourself in a crowded rink required mental preparation too. For open ice rinks are quasi-anarchist states. Danger is everywhere. Reckless skaters amuse themselves by weaving in and out of packs of people to land axel jumps; to avoid being 'it,' kids play tag against the collective skating current; in every direction roughhousing teens fly by like kamikazes, crashing into sidewalls to stop, harming themselves and the friends they target.

When people started gathering around the sidewall closest to the lake, I figured one of the kamikazes landed a direct hit on a bystander. More curious than concerned, I went over to assess the damage. When I did, I realized I was mistaken. It was no kamikaze. The eyes of the crowd were drawn beyond the rink where the sun beamed through the snow-dusted pines all the way to the lake. Yet while the image was certainly picturesque, mother nature itself was too subtle a beauty to demand the immediate attention of city folk accustomed to the instant gratifications of places like Times Square.

"What am I missing," I asked the lady next to me.

"There's a man out there," she said.

Before I could ask 'where,' I saw him.

A skater glided out from a bend in the trees and zoomed toward the far side of the lake. The upper jaws of sunlight and the lower jaws of the horizon line swallowed him at the distant vanishing point. The Park made it clear that lake-skating was prohibited. Every few feet, a sign was posted saying so.

All of us caged in that little ice rink, going round and round, regulated by cones and teenage security staff and turn-styles, went home feeling a little foolish that day. While we shared this tiny artificial space with what felt like the entire borough of

Brooklyn, one man right next to us enjoyed a lake to himself, sharing only with the sun and the trees and the developing stars.

I knew, and I think everyone else did too, that we were not looking at a law-breaker. We were looking at freedom.

8

The Daughter of the Library of Alexandria

The library in the Serapeum, aka the Daughter of the Library of Alexandria, would be smoke and bodies before morning. If the Roman soldiers and Christian mobs worked better together, us heathens, us polytheistic worshippers of Serapis, would die sooner than that.

Thankfully, their collective fury impinged on their efforts to organize, delaying their inevitable breach of our barricades. At least that's what I thought. Nowadays, I question all my thoughts. It's a side effect of the times, the price for knowing that men killing in the name of their god are not to be underestimated.

Our god—Serapis—was their target. His followers, collateral. You'd think he'd get different treatment than other gods, being that Serapis is an amalgamation of countless other gods, including their own Christian one. But he didn't. We didn't. To the mob and the soldiers supporting them, other gods get no piece of the worshipping pie, even if a god, like Serapis, is a preexisting slice of it. This notion was something they were proud to kill or be killed for. Or at least that's how they phrased it. Truth is, they never did the dying. This old library, doubling as a house of worship, would prove that again tonight.

Yet how heroic they'd make the slaughter sound.

I'm sure one of the bards among them was already drafting the victory song. If all sides passed their own purity test, it would be easier to digest. But they don't. Most men fight for gods like they fight for kings. Because they have to. Because there is no alternative. Because when a sword is coming down on you either way, your chances are better if you accept a weapon to deflect the blow instead of asking for a chopping block to rest your neck. In other words, not everyone who bows their head before a statue or fights in the name of a god does so on the back of religious devotion. Many are pinned by the alternative.

Otherwise, they end up like us, trapped in a library doubling as a house of worship, listening to the mob bang away at the massive statue of Serapis in the courtyard, fast reducing him to a pile of rubble on the patio floor. Once he's swept away, they will come for us. And when they do, they will not engage us with the great gift of human intellect, which this room, this great library, was built to host. No, instead they'll engage with sharp pieces of metal, modern adaptations of claws brandished by beasts who can't create history.

Here it comes.

A flurry of flaming arrows whooshed by in the dark, ultimately lodging into an old bookshelf. In came another wave. Then another. And another, until fire eclipsed darkness, summoning the enemy on foot.

When the first man busted through the barricade, I thought to myself, *it's time to meet my maker—be it Christ, Serapis... whoever.*

How will it happen? By ax? Sword? Spear? Some other modern claw?

Hopefully not by bow. Arrows, especially the flaming ones, are so impersonal. I want my slayer, the one who kills me for my "beliefs," to feel my death, to endure me thrusting their own blade deeper into me than intended so I'm skewered far enough to coo this plea into his ear.

"For Christ or Serapis, have mercy on the books behind me. They are the only chance... for all of us."

9

The Last Ride

When Lonny heard the whistle, he put his belly on the ground and turned his head to the mountains. From there, he had the best spot to watch the train descend into the valley.

The conductor was first to pass. He drove the locomotive like a dog sits in a car—with a big smile on his face and his head out the window. Lonny returned the conductor's joy like always, with an enthusiastic wave and an even bigger smile back. When the passengers in the cabin cars came next, he gave the same salutation; as he did with the businessmen in the dining car reading the *Chicago Tribune* who followed; and to the three engineers working on the exterior of the caboose.

Lonny loved the engineers. Armed with modest hand tools, he delighted in how they spent their days watching the world roll away in reverse, fixing whatever problem the moving train encountered next. To Lonny, engineers were machine doctors, borderline superheroes. One day, he hoped to join their noble calling.

Key word—one day. Today, he did not want to be one of the engineers.

Despite what Lonny had always been told—to never drive the train above medium because it increased engine strain and decreased train lifespan—he pushed the joystick on the remote to full-throttle. Decrease the train's lifespan? What difference did lifespan make now? After today, the train would be gone. It deserved to go out in a blaze of glory.

Acting on that idea, Lonny forced his trembling hand to grab the lever next to the track and pull down the railroad switch. The train changed course at the next junction. Rather than take its typical route into a tiny town station, it redirected toward a series of orange and white-striped barricades with blinking red lights. The extra oomph of full throttle made the impediments falter in the face of the train's cow plow. The larger bulwarks split in half. The smaller ones deflected onto the ballast or turned to dust. Now only space and empty track lay between train and table's edge.

The crash was louder than Lonny expected.

Amidst a sea of sparks, the locomotive disconnected from the other cars and slid across the oak floor, stopping only when it smashed into the trim around the door. Those on board suffered unfortunate fates. The conductor flew out the window; the passengers lay prostrate on beds of glass underneath their flipped cabin cars; the businessmen huddled under the white linens draped over the communal tables, their copies of the *Chicago Tribune* fluttering about the car like oversized birds in an undersized aviary. And the engineers? Gone. Nowhere to be found.

In another room, Lonny's mom was hot and sick of reading. She tackled both problems by rolling up her magazine and fanning her face. Roy took her actions to mean she welcomed conversation. Unfortunately for Roy, the crash in the back, and Lonny's subsequent cries occurred before he could capitalize on the flirting opportunity.

Both adults ran into the next room. Roy followed an audible trail of whimpers to a spot underneath the back table. There he found Lonny, with remote control clutched in hand, wailing about engineers.

"I'm so sorry, Roy," Lonny's mom said as she ran for the broom behind the cash register.

Roy beat her to it, assuring her with a smile that it was okay. With that accomplished, he walked over to the locomotive still smoking against the wall and did what he did best—tinker.

A few tugs at the engine wires and a blow from his compressed air container brought it back to life again.

"Something for our best customer to remember us by," Roy said, handing wet-faced Lonny the locomotive they both adored. "Also, I met these men on my way back from the broom closet. They say they are looking for work."

The next day, "Roy's Model Trains and Tracks" closed its doors forever. The engineers are still working.

10

Allies

J anice ran her sponge back and forth over the melting dots of whipped cream until her elbow burned and the bamboo tabletop sparkled. When she took on a second job as a Starbucks barista, she thought it would be an easy way to supplement her income. In hindsight, that decision failed to consider how tired she was of picking up after people. Middle age will do that to you. So will kids. So will divorce.

Most of the time, Janice coped with these, and other, frustrations. Yet every so often, her internal turmoil boiled over onto customers. Or, as in this case, onto poser customers.

"Excuse me, sir, I don't think you purchased that cup of coffee from here," Janice said to Alexander, the man sitting at the table next to the one she just finished scrubbing.

Rather than respond, Alexander began pounding away on his computer keys, believing the busier he looked, the less the woman with the Janice nametag would bother him. Plus, loud typing beat coming to terms with the old barista's accusations. Simply put, Janice was right. Alexander wasn't drinking coffee.

Armed with an empty Starbucks cup from his car, he was faking it for the Wi-Fi.

"Excuse me, sir, I don't think you purchased that cup of coffee," Janice repeated herself, well-trained in handling people ignoring her.

"Prove it, Janice," Alexander finally said. He knew going straight for the 'Janice' instead of the gentler 'Miss' or 'Mam' meant war, and he was enough on the defensive to wage it. "Prove I didn't buy anything."

"Show me your receipt?" Janice said.

"Nobody gets receipts," Alexander said.

"What did you order?" Janice asked.

"Black coffee. Dark Roast," Alexander replied.

"Method of payment?" Janice hissed.

"Why?" Alexander snarled.

"So I can check the transaction history," Janice said, regaining her composure.

"I paid cash," Alexander said, doing the same.

"Time of purchase?" Janice asked.

"This morning," Alexander replied.

Janice turned to the clock on the wall. It was 11:55 am.

"Ma'am, won't you please just leave him alone," a middle-aged white man in a suit and tie said as he snapped the store copy of the *Wall Street Journal* to the next page from a nearby table. *Ugh*, Janice thought, his smug air of superiority brought her ex to mind. So did his clumsiness. While lowering the newspaper to his lap, he caught the wire of his phone charger in the opinion pages, causing the plug to catapult from the wall outlet to within striking distance of his coffee.

Janice wished the near miss had been a direct hit. If the middle-aged white man was reduced to screaming about stained shirts and spilled coffee, his allegiance to Alexander would change from asset to liability. Presently, however, he served as a formidable ally from the establishment. She hated to admit it, but their allegiance drained some of her assertiveness.

"Yeah, you really have no right to treat him like that," a young woman with piercings and pink hair chimed in from the next table over. Her exhibitionist style and her fortified position behind a wall of science textbooks gave away her college student status. Unlike the girl, Janice didn't go to college; she also didn't dye her hair. She delegated that to the aging process. And while she did have two piercings, they were limited to the unimaginative middle of each earlobe.

These stark contrasts made Janice fear the college girl like she feared the middle-aged white man in the suit. Together, as Alexander's allies, they were too much to handle. A white flag waved in her mind.

"I'm on to you, mister," Janice said in a hushed, defeated tone toward Alexander. Then she retreated behind the cash register with her soapy hands inside her green apron.

"What a bitch," the college girl said, putting down one of her books to sip from her plastic Starbucks travel mug. "At least you made the effort to grab something with Starbucks on it before you came in. Other people don't even bother."

"You don't think I bought my coffee here?" Alexander asked.

"Maybe a few months ago, but not recently. The stains on the side of the cup are aged," the college girl said.

"They're also too light for black coffee," the white man in the suit reading the *Wall Street Journal* said as he packed up.

"Do you even have anything in there?" the college girl asked.

"I finished right before Janice started her accusations," Alexander said.

"Sure you did," the college girl said. "Here, let me fill your cup with some of mine. I insist."

"That really isn't necessary," Alexander said. Yet when he removed the lid of his Starbucks cup at the same time as saying this, his actions spoke louder than words. The college girl poured coffee from her plastic Starbucks travel mug into his paper Starbucks cup.

"Now that's black coffee," the white man in the suit reading the *Wall Street Journal* said as parting words while he watched the college girl pour. When he exited the store shortly there-after, the store copy of the newspaper was rolled up under his arm.

"It's really good coffee too," Alexander said after his first sip. "What is it?"

The college girl raised the plastic Starbucks travel mug to her lips with a smile. "Dunkin."

11

Bfftdl

Barnes marched five paces out from the boxcar lodged against the subway tunnel wall, then he dropped his duffel bag packed with steaks and bent down to unsheathe the nearest railroad spike from its ballast hole. As the carved teeth in the bottom portion of the steel indicated upon its exit from a sleeve in the ground, this was no longer a railroad spike. It was a key.

Barnes jigged the key into the boxcar keyhole until it unlocked. The door, now ajar, opened into a corridor that led underneath the current level of tunnels. Barnes followed the corridor to a large room with dimensions like a school gymnasium. The only lights inside hung from the central ceiling beams, the result being a spotlight effect on the gravel ring taking up the middle of the room.

Everywhere else was darkness.

"Barnes, out of the way," George yelled from the cab enclosure of his forklift. The frantic tone of the maintenance man was caused by what he was carrying. A large hairy hominid, twice the bulk of a guerilla and double the height of a standing grizzly bear, paced in a cage above the carriage, anticipating his exit into the ring. Meet Mucho. Reigning champ.

After George lowered Mucho's cage to the ground and released his forks from its cargo, he passed Barnes again, this time to pick up Gus, the challenger.

Gus was another subspecies of sasquatch, smaller than Mucho, but blessed with an exceptional tapetum lucidum, an eye feature that enhanced his night-vision. Given this feature, Gus saw Barnes sitting alone in the darkest perimeter of the quasi-gymnasium, ass-out on an old loose railroad tie, when nobody else did. Barnes seemed to know the squatch was watching him, for he made some manual body articulations back in Gus's direction.

Gus watched Barnes in his peripheral until the bell sounded and the cage doors swung open, sending Mucho charging.

Boom. Boom. Boom.

One heavy blow after another hit Gus like cannon fire, sending the undersized squatch out of the ring and into the darkness. His pride kept him coming back for another pounding, sometimes from Mucho's fist, other times from kicks, elbows, or knees. Yet the repetition bored the champion. Mucho grew frustrated. Tired of waiting for Gus to come to him, he went to Gus in the darkness.

Thankfully, the champion's pursuit of the challenger in darkness did not impact the visual experience of the spectators. The drone following the fighters and live-streaming the event worldwide had night vision capabilities. On camera, the light to dark transition was barely noticeable. The same couldn't be said for Mucho. The giant hominid, becoming more bold and more reckless with every step away from the gravel ring, started to see very little. Soon his only reference point, his only guiding light, came from the ring, which was fast becoming a fading star. Beginning to get desperate, Mucho started swinging his massive arms around like a peasant cutting grass with a scythe, hoping more with every second that his huge fists would clip Gus one too many times and end the match by knockout.

It didn't work out that way.

Eventually, Mucho did find Gus. When he did, the challenger easily ducked and barrel-rolled away from the punches upon him, grabbed a railroad spike, and jammed it into the champion's foot. While Mucho struggled to spring loose, Gus reached for something bigger. Leaning against the wall was a steel rail, double the size of a baseball bat. Gus picked it up and whacked Mucho's head like a ball on a tea. Two swings later, the undefeated champion's brains were soup in a bowl of gravel.

Shock struck the digital world. Gus was the new champion of the "No Disqualifications, Gladiatorial Rules" division of the "Big Foot Fight to the Death League" (BFFTDL).

Winning didn't make the sasquatch happy. No large hominids care for fighting. A gentle race, they do the deed because they are forced to, because they have no choice. Barnes, who also hated the BFFTDL, felt the same way about his own position as head veterinarian of the league. In vet school, he believed the foremost expert on sasquatches had options beyond being a glorified cut man for the BFFTDL. How naïve.

"You feeling okay?" Barnes signed to Gus as he brought over the first round of steaks from his duffle bag. Such signing was done in an encrypted sign language that Barnes developed and only the two of them knew.

"I'll be better when I'm studding," Gus signed back in their subtle encrypted language.

"Point taken. I'll go talk to management," Barnes signed back as he turned to walk away.

Gus grunted, making Barnes face the new champion once more.

"Thanks for the spike," Gus signed. "And the rail."

12

Birthday Wishes

"Happy birthday to you. Happy birthday to you. Happy birthday Dear Dahlia..."

Dahlia hoped they would stop.

"Are you one, are you two..."

They didn't.

"Make a wish!" a boy yelled from the other end of the table.

"Yeah, make a wish," his friends echoed behind him.

Dahlia hurried to blow out the candles. The sooner she did, the sooner the group of boys could get their cake, jump back in the pool, and stop torturing her. Their afternoon of misbehavior proved some kids just weren't ready for their first boy-girl party.

A little girl's arm tugged at Dahlia's sundress. "What'd you wish for?"

"You know she can't share her wish, honey," an older woman's voice said. "Or it won't come true."

Dahlia's aversion for patronizing adults made her want to answer the little girl's question. All that kept her from doing so was the nature of the wish itself. All Dahlia wanted, all she wished for, was to keep her clothes on, to stay dry, to keep her body out of a bathing suit.

Old enough now to know that wishes are unreliable, Dahlia made efforts to delay her fears from coming true. Superstitions worked for most of the afternoon. While food was out, she could blame digestion for staying out of the water. Yet with lunch over and the cake fleeing fast from the platter, those excuses were numbered. Desperate for an extra insurance policy, Dahlia grabbed one of the few remaining slices.

Her mother wasn't having it.

"Dahlia, before you eat another piece please see if Tess wants some."

Tess was the pool party lifeguard, hired as much for her swimming prowess as for her relationship to the family. Tess was Dahlia's older sister's best friend.

Also, Tess was perfect. And for that reason, she did not eat cake.

"I'm still working on the fruit salad," Tess said, using the side of her mouth unobstructed by her red whistle to respond to Dahlia's offer. Then, with a slight point of her finger, she directed Dahlia to the berry bowl between her toes.

"You aren't getting off that easy on my birthday. I'm getting the cool whip to top you off," Dahlia said, wondering whether a year of squats could transform her lower-half into anything like the one in front of her.

From the dessert table across the pool, her mother, holding a pair of brown shopping bags in each hand, gave a shout. "Dahlia honey, I'll take care of Tess. Go put one of these on. Time to join everyone in the pool!"

Dahlia grabbed the bags from her mother and stomped into the pool house. Once inside, she emptied the bags into a pile on the couch. Compliments of her mother, she had multiple styles and sizes to choose from, even a one piece, which was tempting, but ultimately cast aside for a modest bikini. Dahlia figured they'd torture her no matter what she wore, so she might as well be bold about it.

After undressing, she looked at her nuggety body in the mirror. Unlike the tan, toned legs of Tess, Dahlia had white and flabby... and hairy, tree trunks. Why did her cruel mother forbid her from shaving until middle school? What difference did a month make? At least it would have solved one problem.

Until she could consult a plastic surgeon behind her mother's back, she wasn't solving a bigger (or really smaller) problem: her chest. She pushed her bikini top together so her nipples touched—flat as a board. *The only place I don't have fat is the one place I want it... Whatever. Let's get this over with,* Dahlia said to herself, returning the unselected bathing suits to the bag and heading toward the pool house doors. *If things go as badly as expected, I can always go to private school.*

A loud crack came from the sky. Tess's red lifeguard whistle screamed. Then Tess did herself:

"Lightning. Everyone out of the pool."

13

Evening Tones

Vaughn's insomnia was the best part of moving to Queens. Every night, he'd lay in bed and watch the ceiling, waiting for the music to start, wondering what instrument the musician upstairs would summon that evening.

A time and a place; however, exists for everything. Besides Vaughn, most tenants believed the time and place for recitals was during the day. At night, adults needed sleep for work; kids needed sleep for school. They emphasized those points when they stormed the musician's door demanding silence. Sometimes it worked. Sometimes it didn't.

When it didn't, Yost the landlord came knocking.

That never ended well. In fact, it never really ended at all. Unlike the tenants, who the musician gave the dignity of an open door, Yost engaged in one-sided conversation with the wall until he grew so tired from his own squawking that he fell asleep right there on the landing. By the time this occurred, the sun was up, and the building was so sick of Yost that they hoped the musician would drown him out with the very tunes they'd tried to silence a few hours ago.

Vaughn was no exception. When Yost came for rent the next morning, his face still indented from the hallway carpet upstairs, he felt like giving him the silent treatment perfected by his upstairs neighbor.

"Your yelling is a nuisance. I should withhold this," Vaughn said, giving in, and slapping a wad of cash into the landlord's hand.

"No. No. Don't do that. I'm terribly sorry. I've been dealing with some really selfish tenants," Yost said loudly, hoping his voice carried up the steps. Disappointed by no reaction from upstairs, the landlord went back to counting bills and spreading musician gossip. The dirty secrets he dished out were details that only a lover could know, and only an ex-lover could say.

Perhaps by coincidence, perhaps in reaction to the land-lord's last trumpeted comments, heavy footsteps trounced across the floor above their heads.

A door opened.

An extraterrestrial wearing a paisley top, Gucci sunglasses, and Neiman Marcus platform pumps came downstairs, passed Vaughn and Yost in the hallway, and went out onto the sidewalk with a reusable Trader Joe's grocery bag swinging from her shoulder.

Anticipating chaos, Vaughn ran to the window to watch the world respond. He didn't get the show he expected. Queens, it turned out, treated aliens like any other local: some folks waved; others nodded; some, like one teenage girl, ran up and hugged them. Everyone else, focused on phones and friends and picking up dog poop, paid no attention.

"Why do you let her stay?" Vaughn asked.

"Grandfathered in," Yost said.

"How does she pay rent?"

"Worst way possible," Yost said, turning to the window himself. "Music lessons."

14

Multiculturalism

The newspaper in the hotel lobby had doubled in size since yesterday. So it was Sunday. I never thought I'd see a Sunday in Mississippi. My travels took me to strange places.

Those strange places had strange people. Three of them sat at the table next to me. The oldest of their lot, and seemingly the most vulnerable to fresh trays of sausage gravy and biscuits, did not stay seated for long. His trek across the laminate floor gave me my first look at the rattail. Like he was striking a pose, he twirled the gray little devil between his fingers until it was tight as a joint and greasy as a pan of bacon. Then back behind his neck it went, slithering under the collar of his cut-sleeve Sturgis shirt so he could fill the waffle maker without fear of a (hair) fire hazard.

It beeped when it shut, alarming the old man with the rattail.

"Just twist it like I showed you, stud," a little white woman said from back at the table. Based on her age and her apparel— she wore a "Redneck Princess" tee-shirt — she was his wife.

Their son was the shirtless man sitting next to her. His "Redneck Princess" upper back tattoo, captioned "Momma's Boy," eliminated any doubt of that fact. Other family body art confirmed he had children as well as a mother. A pair of baby footprints were tattooed on each tricept. Each footprint contained a printed name inside the heel. Another tattoo marked his waistline. The longhorn belt buckle holding up his baggy jean-shorts shielded most of its contents, rendering it unidentifiable.

Click-clack. Heels marched across the tile floor. I turned my head instinctively in search of eye candy. When I did, I found a thick black woman in business professional attire beelining for the breakfast buffet. Two girls in matching pleated skirts trailed her to the waffle iron.

A minute later, it started beeping again.

"You have to turn it," the old man with the rattail counseled from the table. For further guidance, he was kind enough to act out his instructions while talking.

"I know I've got to turn it," the thick black woman said. "But I only have two arms. I can't flip the waffle iron and make three plates at once. Maybe Mr. Skin sitting next to you can help out."

"Sorry, Melis... zoned out there for a minute," the shirtless man said as he ran to help with the plates and the pile of waffles growing on top of them. When he held all he could carry, he brought the goods back to his parents' table where three more chairs were already added so all six of them could sit together: the old man with the rattail; his wife with the Redneck Princess t-shirt; the shirtless son; Melissa; and the two little girls.

"Can't we just go to a later mass?" the shirtless man said.

"The girls have games later," Melissa replied.

"I think I know that," the shirtless man said back. "I'm the coach."

"Not a very good one according to your record," she chirped.

The old man with the rattail chuckled at Melissa's retort and reached for a hand-pound.

"Also, where's your shirt?" Melissa asked the shirtless man. "Seriously?"

"I just got out of the pool. Gimme the room key and I'll change," he said.

Melissa reached into her chic little purse and handed over the plastic swipe-card. The shirtless took the card, pecked each girl on the check, and planted a wet one on Melissa's mouth. Then he stretched his arms above his head, making the previously unidentifiable lower stomach tattoo climb over his longhorn belt buckle and become identifiable. All it said, in familiar Allman Brother's record vinyl font, was "Sweet Melissa."

"He's a lucky man," the Redneck Princess said to the old man with the rattail. "What do you think about your daughter-in-law grandpa?"

"I think the men in this family know how to pick 'em," the man with the rattail said as he smiled and winked at both granddaughters.

15

The Orange File of Mr. Conroir

"He's late for his two pm," I said when I reached Becky's desk behind the reception window.

"I'm surprised you even picked up the file," she said as she leaned back in her chair and tied back her greying hair.

"Who's next?" I asked, peering into the waiting room to scout the patient pool. Becky slipped a blue file into my hand as I did so.

Blue files are for new patients.

"Harley Varons, age forty-three," I said to myself as I shut my office door. Before looking at the photo ID stapled to the inside cover of the blue folder, I guessed the face in the crowded waiting room that matched that name. When I sat down at my desk and checked my answer, I was pleased with the result. Harley Varons was indeed the man in the corner of the waiting room, huddled over his phone, oblivious to the little yellow-eyed monster coiled up under his chair, snoozing.

Typical of a blue folder file, and unlike the other, more secured, monsters in the waiting room, Harley Varon's monster lacked all signs of domestication: no leash, no muzzle, no cage. Taking him on as a patient meant starting from scratch. No problem. In fact, that was preferable. The alternative— patients familiar with me and/or my type of practice—are too comfortable. They ask too many questions, most of them useless.

I took the blue ballpoint pen from my ear and jotted down a rough plan for our time together. Based on similar cases, eight sessions with Harley Varons should do it, set to occur in the following fashion:

Meetings 1-2:Learn to feed monster on schedule.

Meeting 2-3: Obedience School I: Collar and leash monster. Take for walk.

Meetings 4-5:Obedience School II: Positive Reinforcement for good behavior.

Meetings 6-7:Radical Acceptance: Must domesticate. Cannot slay.

Meeting 8: Maintenance practices/Preventative Prep for relapse

THE INTERCOM SOUNDED WHEN I FINISHED WRITING.

"He's here," Becky said.

I kept her on speaker for a moment before responding: "But it's almost three."

"He called earlier this week to reschedule from two to three. I forgot all about the change," Becky said.

I plowed my fingers over the top of my scalp and breathed to the extent my pounding heart allowed.

"Send him in," I finally said, looking at the clump of hair now piled up in my hand.

After Becky hung up, I set Mr. Varon's blue file to the side and unlocked my bottom desk drawer, where I kept the biggest file in my office— the orange file of Mr. Conroir.

Why is it the biggest file in my office? Because Mr. Conroir is my monster.

On days I can't face him alone, thank god for Becky.

16

Tangled

I sat alone in a secluded section of the library. I enjoyed it here. Like a little fortress, the stacks that surrounded me provided ample cover for munching on my peanut butter sandwich, a prohibited act in a place proud to post signs at every corner that warned, "Libraries are for reading, not eating." Perhaps because it nearly rhymed, especially when you made the 't' in 'eating' sound like a 'd' (that is to say, "Libraries are for reading, not eading") it became a staff slogan. Employees recited it like teenagers singing overplayed pop songs.

Each bite of my peanut butter sandwich tasted better when I considered it a gesture in defiance of them and their crafty little nursery rhyme.

A girl approached my table with the plug of her computer cord in hand. Coward that I was, I threw my sandwich in my backpack to bury the evidence of my wrongdoing.

"Can I share your outlet?" she said, not noticing my rule breaking.

"Be my guest," I replied.

I used the time she spent hunched over the outlet as an opportunity to wipe away any residue of my peanut butter piggery. I achieved that goal within a few runs of the sleeve across my face, at which point I was much more presentable, and much harder to accuse of breaking the golden library rule.

"Lose something?" I asked after watching her burrow through her backpack after plugging in the cord.

"Yeah, my last piece of butterscotch," she said in a muffled tone, her head still halfway in the bag.

"No luck?" I asked.

Her full head resurfaced with a satisfied smile. An orange candy wrapper was in her hand. "Not until now," she replied.

I found that cute. The mousy noises her mouth made while sucking was cute too.

"Left my iPhone charger at home. You have one I could borrow?" she asked.

"You sure have a lot of plug problems today," I said, regretting the words once I said them.

Interpreting her silence as confusion, I grabbed my iPhone charger out of my bag and said, "Sure. But it's going to take two to untangle." This play on words of the cliché "two-to-tango" achieved less than desired comedic effect.

She smiled, probably more to applaud my effort rather than because I was funny. Either way, it worked. Right after I said the corny line, she came over and sat next to me. Six o'clock fast turned to seven-thirty. Our laughter showed no signs of stopping. The charger, however, remained untangled, a fact she brought to my attention when she rose for a cigarette break.

Smitten, and growing shameless as a result, I asked to kiss her before she left.

She agreed.

Looking back, she probably shouldn't have.

Her face swelled. Her throat tightened. My tongue went from twirling to trapped. My mind recalled that aggravating slogan: "The library is for reading, not eating."

Peanuts.

17

Sunglasses

A network of suspension footbridges guided my trek over the bog. They came equipped with signs that explained the local flora and fauna inhabiting the area. Each time I reached a sign, I made of game of it to read the poster and see how much of what it referenced I could find from my spot on the footbridge. Noticing my sunglasses were now a hindrance with the declining sun, I flipped them above my brow.

Then I slung the upper half of my body over the suspension footbridge and gazed into the water, this time in color.

Splash.

Expensive, new, sentimental value, birthday present, these words and phrases flooded my mind as I watched my sunglasses submerge into the muddy water like a tiny submarine. Leaving them to Davy Jones's locker didn't even cross my mind. The sunglasses meant too much to me. I had to go down and get them.

One step onto the bank below the suspended footbridge. That's all it took to realize what relaxed me up there made my mind race down here. When you get up close and personal with it, nature is like that a lot. One moment you are on top of a bridge, a human engineering marvel, looking over your dominion from what might as well be the clouds. Then you are down in the mud, where at every turn, something jumps, and whatever the size, it makes you jump. In my case, it also convinced me to keep my clothes on for additional protection as I started wading into the water.

One step in, and the soft leafy bottom of the creek flooded my Birkenstocks.

A few more steps in, the water deepened, and the mud increased its suction. Everything icky. Everything so slimy to the touch.

AHHH!

Pain shot into my right calf. My ass fell into the water.

What I deemed the work of a water moccasin turned out to be the partially submerged branch of a thorny tree. Based on my reading the sign on the suspension footbridge above, I knew my attacker: the honey locust.

A large Egret fishing the shallows shook its head at me in disgust. I didn't appreciate the gesture. If I had pipe-cleaner legs the size of stilts to poke around the bog, I'd thrive in this environment too. But I didn't. I had to get along with lululemon shorts and Birkenstocks. And I had to find those sunglasses. $500 frames aren't as dispensable as minnows.

So, I continued on, deeper and deeper into the bog, until I got right under the middle of the bridge where I'd dropped the sunglasses. By now, the bottom composition of the bog had changed, going from grimy to sandy. Initially, I appreciated the change. Then I got to thinking... whatever lurked on a clean bottom did not need cover.

My feet ran over something smooth yet slimy and ridged,

and therefore out of place. My gut said rock. My mind said snapping turtle. For the sake of my toes, I was glad to conclude, upon further investigation, that my gut was correct. It was a rock.

A few more steps in the opposite direction of the rock, I again felt something that didn't belong to this bottom. This time though, that something could not be mistaken for a creature capable of executing my phalanges, or a creature at all for that matter. The something was hard plastic with a mechanical feel. That something was my sunglasses.

Too tired to make a fire by the time I got back to the campsite, I elected for a quick sandwich, a hand sanitizer bath, and the inside of my sleeping bag instead. Before proceeding with that agenda, I undressed, piling my smelly clothes just outside the tent, denying them further entry.

I woke up a few hours later, likely because the stars shined so bright through my tent that my body mistook it for morning. For an unobstructed view, I unzipped the tent and went outside. Pursuit of the stars came at a price:

I forgot my sunglasses were still inside my lululemon shorts, and my shorts were...

Crunch.

18

Interstate

"Want anything, Herb?" Charlie asked, opening the passenger door.

"Coffee," Herb muttered as he slid the keys from the ignition and puffed smoke out the driver's side window.

"Frankie?" Charlie asked.

"Coming," Frankie said, sliding out from her scrunched-up position in the middle seat and joining Charlie on the pavement.

Herb watched Frankie and Charlie flash in and out of the parking lot streetlights on their way toward the entrance to the State Welcome Center. Only when the doors opened and let them inside did his fingers leave his holster for his cigarette.

"Hey, Anika? How are you? We'll have two number tens and a large coffee please," Charlie said to the old Indian woman working the register at the Welcome Center eatery.

"Herb isn't hungry?" Anika asked with a customary smile.

"Herb sticks to coffee at this time of night, Anika, you know that. No need to mind your manners with us. Save it for the stiffs."

"You both look tired," Anika said. "Get off your feet. I'll bring the food to the usual spot."

Their order contained double what they asked for and included a few extra apple pies and some soft serve ice cream. Anika was always good for the add-ons. She brushed off her kindness as gossip currency. By delivering Charlie and Frankie the goods, she could stick around for a while without feeling like an imposition. While they appreciated the extras, such insecurities were unfounded. Despite working very different jobs, the three women were kindred spirits.

"Can I get you anything else?" Anika asked when she got up after getting her desired few minutes of chit chat.

"You have any antiseptic? My blisters are bad," Charlie asked, only half-joking. She knew from experience that Anika's purse was a pharmacy.

"Fortunately, I get to wear comfortable shoes in my line of work. So no. But I'll ask around," Anika said.

"Forget it," Charlie replied. "We'll be home in a few hours. I have stuff there."

Frankie was still digging for chicken nuggets on their way back to the van. "We did well tonight," she said, barely understandable with so much food in her mouth. This was the one time of the week they pigged out. Knowing all too well that when the sun came up, their spartan routines returned for the week, Frankie took full advantage of that.

"We always do well," Charlie said while shoving a few final fries in her mouth, equally aware of the time constraints for their gluttony.

By the time they reached Charlie's townhouse, specks of

sun crept over the hills. The only thing still black was Herb's coffee.

Herb put the van in park and pulled three stacks of cash from his briefcase. A stack went to Charlie. A stack went to Frankie. A stack stayed with him.

"Until next weekend, friends," Charlie said, taking her stack and exiting the vehicle. Herb waited until Charlie got inside before he and Frankie drove off.

Charlie had the shower on before the hum of the van's engine was out of earshot. The mirror began to fog. Before she lost her reflection entirely, she undressed and performed a quick body exam.

"Not bad," she thought to herself. Aside from a few red blotches from slaps and squeezes, and a slight residual sting from last Thursday's Brazilian, everything looked pretty good— perky too. Skin tone was her only concern. In winter, a white person shouldn't be so tan.

To be fair, a lot of her 'color' washed down the shower drain. In fact, when the water hitting off her body went from brown slush back to clear, she knew it was time to get out.

On her way toward her bedroom, Charlie was already planning what to wear. More than anything else, she hated having to linger in her closet. Being inside of it brought back memories of playing 'house' as a little girl—with one huge difference. In those days, the closet of her imagination contained blazers, pant suits, pencil skirts, and the like. At present, Charlie's real-life closet was a den of G-strings, law enforcement costumes, assless chaps, and platform high heels.

When she'd started stripping in college, it was a means to an end, a way to save money for grad school and maintain financial independence, both of which were central to her liberation as a woman. Now thirty, Charlie had degrees without debt; an unmortgaged townhouse; and a successful business with a van and two employees: Herb the bookkeeper/bouncer, and Frankie, her fellow female stripper. With those original goals achieved, the time had come to start another one.

Tomorrow, Charlie was shopping for pantsuits.

19

The Space Bus to Oslphintror

R awatek was the first prisoner offered the opportunity to take the space bus to Oslphintror. He earned that chance after 200 years in Huilthi prison, all on good behavior, in an era of rapid advancements in anti-aging science. When Rowatek entered prison, a male of his species from the planet Zivoso had a 175-year life expectancy. The day the sun shined down on him for the first time on the free side of Huilthi, Zivoson males like Rowatek routinely reached age 1000.

Penal systems were unequipped for so long a custody arrangement. To handle this new reality, changes were needed. Putting Rawatek on a Universal Transit Authority (UTA) space bus bound for Oslphintror was one of them.

"Please explain your dress?" one of the reporters standing by the UTA bus asked, curious to hear why Rawatek was wearing all green garb from head to foot.

"Oslphintror will be a new beginning based on anonymity. We don't want what you *were*. We want what you *are*," Rawatek explained, fully hidden behind the green garb.

"And the color?" another reporter yelled out.

"Green indicates growth," Rawatek replied. Then, without another word, he stepped away from the cameras, boarded the UTA bus, and was off to Oslphintror... never to be seen again.

Today, it's essentially Oslphintrorian law to fully shroud oneself in "Rawatek Green." In fact, to be uncovered, to reveal yourself in public, puts your life in jeopardy. Strict as these and other rules are, Oslphintror attracted more than paroled super-criminals and fugitives seeking sanctuary. Crime-tourists, intrigued by the idea of walking amongst notorious fugitives and criminals of universe-wide renown, came in droves, as did those seeking their own form of spiritual enlightenment amongst the fellow sufferers.

Whatever reason they came, they did so in spite of the infamous solo-traveler rule, which was: everyone who traveled to Oslphintror travelled alone. And for the most part, they came like Rawatek—by UTA space bus.

Sure, even to Oslphintror, more glamorous methods of travel existed. But such methods eroded tradition. Plus, when pilgrims took the Space Bus, it also served a practical purpose. The guilty could blend in with the non-guilty. In practice, this meant that the second someone in the green garb who entered a UTA Space Bus, be them tourist, parolee, fugitive, spiritual seeker, or the like, were generally safe from police suspicion all the way to Oslphintror. As long as they kept their mouth shut, the world left them alone.

I began my journey to the land of the green garb from the far side of the universe. So I had ample time as the center of attention aboard my respective UTA space bus. The whole time, even when other passengers weren't looking at me, they were looking at me. Their silence made their swallowed questions louder than screams. Who are you? Why are you going?

Even if they had the guts to ask a potentially dangerous criminal these questions, it was pointless to do so. Those bound for Oslphintror always answer such questions with the same response. Everyone knew that.

Well, almost everyone.

A child escaped from his mother's arms and ran across the space bus aisle to my seat. The child's mother ran after him in terror. She was too late.

"Why are you going to Oslphintror?" the child asked.

I bent down with a patience that could have been faked by a tourist or honed from hundreds of years behind bars. Then I said what we all said:

"Why one goes to Oslphintror stays between the person and the veil."

20

Silence was the Sound of the Night

"*****No Overnight Guests. ABSOLUTELY No Live-in Girlfriends!!!!!!!!*****

In January, Jackson's roommate Roger had posted that on Craigslist. Jackson had answered the ad with some bullshit line about respecting discipline, and moved in the next week. Now, seven months later, with his ears plugged and his eyes covered by a pillow, that phrase circled the ceiling of his mind like a mobile above a baby crib. Except the mobile of his mind did not play lullabies. It played techno from the room down the hallway.

Did Roger remember that he was breaking his own rule. Probably not. Would he care? Probably not. Before Jackson moved in, Roger had been a virgin. The girlfriend, a late Spring addition, ended that streak the first night she came over. Jackson could attest to that. The end of the streak was apparently the end of the policy.

When the techno turned off, the deed was done. The

thrusts stopped. The springs in the mattress ceased squeaking. Suddenly, silence was the sound of the night.

Based on past experience, intermission wouldn't last. Before long, they'd break their fast and return for a second session, this one lasting until morning. Knowing this, the time to raid the fridge with the least amount of exposure was now.

Jackson made moves.

First, he took the cookies from the hydrator. Then he grabbed his gallon jug of chocolate milk chilling in the side door. The second he grabbed it, he noticed a weight difference between now and his last sip at lunch. Someone else had been imbibing. The list of perps was short. Roger was lactose intolerant. And he didn't have enough of a sweet tooth to agree to the devil's bargain that would come with drinking it. That brought the list down to one.

Clearly the bitch was stealing sips. And it had to stop.

A familiar earthy, floral, woody smoke went up his nose as he closed the refrigerator door, Jackson had kicked his pot smoking fix with the New Year. This post-sex weed-smoking wasn't making the situation any easier. If he wasn't mistaken, the fine-print prohibitions on the infamous craigslist ad had included that too. The hypocrisy from the den of debauchery down the hall just kept on coming.

A cough came from Roger' room.

Jackson craned his neck down the hallway to see if they even had the courtesy to keep the door closed while they blew all that smoke. Apparently not. The door was half-opened. The lights were on. On a large bed with velvet sheets rested a pair of bare legs, strong and slender and shining.

She reached to her right and ashed her blunt in a coffee mug on the floor beside her bed, putting her dangling bare breasts in full view.

"Get a good look, pervert?" she said as she shut the door with her leg and darkened the hallway between them.

Then she screamed, "Roger, hurry up in there. Momma's ready for round two."

Hell of a sister.

21

Ashby

Five-to-one odds, Ashby over Finch in paper football? Not a chance, I thought to myself as I watched Angelo, our school bookie, grab a pad from his locker and log my bet. Should I tell him that he got the odds backward, that it was the other way around, that Finch rather than Ashby should be favored five-to-one?

Nah. Angelo had this coming.

"Finch for $300. I'll have the cash for you after chemistry class," I said.

My confidence in Finch meant no disrespect toward Ashby. Ashby was the phenom before the phenom. As a twenty-year-old learning-disabled, severely dyslexic super-senior, he had skill, steadiness, and experience on his side, which altogether blended into wisdom. Aware of his strengths and limitations, he played within himself, resulting in a conservative style that could be beaten, but only by flawless play. For these reasons, we called him the spider. One mistake stuck you in Ashby's web. After that, it was over. You were spun up and swallowed.

Finch, also known as "the Finger," was a fourteen-year-old paper football phenom with near-superhuman strength in his middle finger, a trait that enabled him to hit shots across cafeteria tables that players before him never even contemplated, let alone landed. The risk in betting on Finch was the volatility of the person himself. An entertainer before a competitor, Finch would rather crowd-please and lose than win and get a victory lap. During a game, that meant taking high-difficulty shots for cheers when less difficult shots were available for wins.

Now a little about our game.

In our version of paper football, two opponents got three flicks or "kicks" with their index or middle fingers toward the opponent's field goal. The field goals were made of the opponents two connected thumbs (the horizontal bar) and two upright fingers (vertical bars). The paper football itself was a folded piece of loose-leaf secured in place by scotch tape.

So, the stage was set for an epic bout. Ashby vs. Finch; "the Spider" vs. "the Finger."

And then chemistry class ended... and I heard the news.

Finch jammed his super finger diving for a ball in gym, rendering it immobile. Based on my calculations, it happened right before I waged my entire summer job savings against Angelo last period.

Normally, one jammed finger is a manageable paper football injury. With limited inconvenience, most players can switch back and forth between fingers. Some players, crafty veterans like Ashby, take it a step further. They aren't just capable of shooting with either finger. They adjust according to shot type, like a golfer changing clubs. Pure power hitters like Finch do not.

To be fair, unlike Ashby, Finch didn't have the liberty to

choose between power and finesse. The freshman phenom had symbrachydactyly, a congenital disease that made him born without a right-hand index finger. As a result, the injury to his right-hand middle finger, combined with his lack of a right index finger rendered him incapable of shooting with his dominant hand. Without an index finger and without present use of his jammed right-hand middle finger, Finch had to shoot with his non-dominant hand. Could he play under those conditions? Sure.

Could he win?

No.

I was going to lose everything.

My only hope was that Ashby wouldn't show. Truancy being his foil, this was always a possibility. It made the consistency of his play less consistent, the number of his victories less voluminous, and the risk of betting on him far higher than it looked on paper. In other words, if Ashby showed up, he usually won. But many times, he never did.

Five minutes of lunch passed without Ashby.

Then ten minutes.

I felt a flicker of hope. But only a flicker. Ashby was late as much as he was MIA, everyone knew that. So, when the crowd began to gather around the largest lunch table stretched halfway across the cafeteria, I figured that was case. In another minute, I confirmed that suspicion. The flicker of hope blew out.

In came Ashby.

He gave a few high-fives. Then he took off his sunglasses and squirted some Visine into his eyes. When he went to give Finch a customary and classy Ashby good-luck handshake, he saw for the first time the bandage around the Finger's finger.

"Fuck this. I'm not playing. The guy is handicapped. Call me when he heals," Ashby said.

22

Opposition to the Engine

Dark. Open. Space. A thin glassy surface below my feet, barely visible in this dark, open, space. I rubbed my eyes to wet them after a long sleep. Where was I?

A loud engine cranked, nay, a loud engine roared. Below my feet, the glassy surface responded to its call and started moving like a giant conveyor belt toward the sound. Dimmers lit the edges on both sides of what I now recognized was a peculiar footbridge. All other surroundings remained unclear. I knew not what the footbridge straddled, what it connected on both sides, or its height above ground.

Yet if I had to guess, I'd say the footbridge was high and long and I was far from either end.

The footsteps of thousands, maybe millions, passed by. Their cloudy eyes and foggy faces paid me no attention. Staying in rhythm with the percussive noise of the distant engine, as well as the footbridge conveyer belt it controlled, enslaved their time, demanded all their focus.

What obedience.

What brainwashing.

For whatever reason, maybe because I just woke-up, I was immune to whatever pull the engine had on all those nearby. Worried my inner agency was on borrowed time from its own enslavement, I did the opposite while I still could. Doing the opposite meant walking in the other direction.

Odd the effects of a little exhibitionism. The second I started my trek I had the attention of all the foggy faces next to me. A few footsteps later, much of that fog lifted, and many turned to follow my lead.

We did not march. We did not walk in unison. But we somehow did it together, in greater unison than the competing foot traffic that kept moving on the conveyor belt toward the engine.

Competing foot traffic didn't last. Before long, a massive domino effect ensued, and everyone on the footbridge turned from whatever fate the engine planned, and embraced their own in the opposite direction. The tug of war between these competing forces on the conveyor belt— the engine on one side, our foot traffic on the other—sent the former into a frenzy.

The engine whined. It screamed. It popped and puttered and stuttered and stopped. And then it roared a final roar before breaking.

Our celebration was short-lived. In moments, the footbridge cracked.

I wondered whether we would fall forever. Then I wondered, would that be so bad? You see, falling, once you've overcome fear of landing, is an amazing thing. You may even call it flying.

23

Civic Duty

Erzi sold me on his "Dine with a Manhattan view" sales pitch. Despite his broken English, he was confident and capable, armed with Broadway cheer and uptown grit. The second he greeted me at the door of the luncheonette, I felt like somebody.

Then Erzi sat me down.

And I felt the window draft. And I knew I'd been banished to the cheap seats, far removed from the only other patron in the store, a large man who sat in the middle of the room where it was warm, ordering course after course, like royalty.

I wished to do the same.

But I didn't act on my wish.

Dripping wet and disheveled from a freezing February rain, I looked unworthy of a better spot. And I didn't have the bankroll to prove otherwise.

"Rain was bound to come at some point. Threatened all day," Erzi said as he clinked some silverware around me, setting my space. "What'll it be?"

To his dismay, I ordered a hot tea with lemon.

"Nothing with it?" Erzi asked. "Maybe something sweet?"

My eyes followed his hand to the hydrator. A colorful selection of sweets decorated two glass shelves. I appreciated the effort to upsell, but declined.

"Just the tea," I said.

His face dropped in disgust. He recovered fast with a smile but not fast enough to hide his true feelings.

On his way back to the counter for my tea, Erzi stopped in front of the large man in the middle of the room. "Anything else, Elliot?"

"Soup on today?" Elliot asked.

"I'll grab you a bowl," Erzi said, hurrying back into the kitchen.

Elliot had his soup long before I had my tea, so I got to watching him. The large man wielded that large wooden spoon like a painter does his brush. He rowed it through the water until his stirs gave him command of the steaming liquid, and his wheezy blows tempered it to taste.

"No good. Take it back," Elliot shouted, spiking the spoon back into the bowl and banging on the table.

Erzi did as Elliot instructed.

"No good. Too hot. Take it back," Elliot said when another soup came out.

"Who are you, fucking Goldilocks?" Erzi said, grabbing Elliot's bowl.

"Well, Goldilocks wants to see a manager or I'm not paying," Elliot said.

Erzi returned from the kitchen with an older version of himself. The man, evidently his father, brought out Elliot's third bowl of soup and slammed it on the table. Apparently, he wanted a front row seat for the next culinary critique, because he dragged a chair next to the large man in a menacing fashion, until their faces were only inches away from one another.

Elliot was unphased. After finishing half the bowl at a leisurely pace, he repeated to the father what he said to the son.

"No good. Too bland. Fix it by the time I get back from the restroom," Elliot said as he snapped his napkin out from over his pants, sending crumbs across the table.

Erzi's father watched Elliot until he disappeared down the hallway toward the sign that said restroom. Then he turned his chair around and faced me.

"I apologize," Erzi's father said with the same disingenuous grin his son had used when I ordered a tea. "But you must leave the store."

By now, I'd seen enough to know he wasn't one to mess with, so I downed another drop of tea and left the Luncheonette. The door locked behind me as soon as my feet hit the sidewalk, leaving only the three of them inside.

Before leaving, I peeked back into the cloudy restaurant window for answers. Erzi and his father were heading toward the restroom. The dining room was empty.

Uneasy and again beginning to get wet, I elected for a seat at the café across the street. I planned to wait it out there until I had visual confirmation of Elliot's exit. Thirty minutes later, and still no Elliot, I began to wonder whether I should call the cops. Two things held me back. One, my knowledge of myself and my tendency to overreact. And two, that I had spent at least half of the last hour buried in my phone texting Lin about plans to meet up.

"I'll be there in a few. I'm a block away!" Lin's last text read.

Five minutes later, she entered the café. When my distraction with the window came at the expense of an enthusiastic hello, she demanded answers. She laughed when I told her.

"You're talking about that place, right?" Lin asked, her finger now pointing across the street to the Luncheonette.

I nodded.

"I eat there all the time. Elliot owns the place with his brother," Lin said. "Erzi is his nephew from overseas. He's training."

24

The Greek God of Gravity

Mack smiled and said hello when Miss McGultry passed his door. Miss McGultry reciprocated in similar fashion, knowing all too well by Mack's lecherous eyes that feasted on her spandex that he and the rest of the local coots would have last night's snowstorm cleared from her car by the time she finished teaching her early morning Pilates class.

Before taking off on her run to get there, Miss McGultry grabbed a piece of mail addressed to Leslie, the cute college girl who'd recently rented the upstairs apartment a door down from Mack, and dropped in the right mailbox. Leslie and Miss McGultry had similar surnames. This likely contributed to the postal error. Oddly enough, they also looked like each other, so much so that if you put a picture of Leslie now next to a picture of Miss McGultry ten years ago, good luck telling them apart.

With the mail deed done, Miss McGultry hit the road on foot. Until the plows lapped the streets a few more times, it was her only method of transport to the gym.

Pilates went well. Like their instructor, the regulars braved the storm for a sweat. No surprise there. With beach season looming, more space existed in between atoms than inside one of Miss McGultry's legendary early morning classes. Her devout students nicknamed her the Greek God of Gravity, possessed with a supernatural skill to eliminate floppy triceps. Clientele of this kind is why Miss McGultry kept the gig. At this point in her life, money troubles were over. Consistent promotion at her 'real' office job ended those anxieties years ago.

Still, mornings like these made her ponder life after being a 'Pilates Instructor.' That wasn't all she pondered about. For a few blocks now, she kept coming back to the same question?

Where were the men? Sure, the snowstorm delayed morning activities to some extent. But that couldn't be all of it.

Where were the men?

She turned onto her street. There, for the first time all morning, she heard the scrape of snow shovels and the plop of slush onto asphalt.

Of course! How could she forget. Men always came around to dig her car out on mornings like these.

Her speculation proved half-right. Indeed, a group of men were shoveling snow off a car. But it was not her car... it was Leslie's.

In a situation like this, some women would convince themselves that the men made a mistake, that they were cleaning the wrong car. Miss McGultry, who faced facts like the earth does the sun, was no such a woman. You couldn't be the Greek God of Gravity and sway from facts. You had to acknowledge truth. You had to accept that your car was still a snowball because your followers worshipped a new deity.

Miss McGultry peered into the nearest car's side mirror, the only part of most vehicles on the street currently uncovered by snow. When she did, water fell from the eyes of her reflection.

Miss McGultry knew this day would come. But so suddenly? All at once? Could one really leave the house in the morning a beautiful young woman and return hours later an undesirable old maid? This transition, and the speed at which it occurred here, could make one weep. Indeed, in the mirror it looked like Miss McGultry was doing just that.

But she wasn't. While she empathized with Leslie, the misfortune of her cute next-door neighbor did not dull her spirits.

Miss McGultry was not crying. She was smiling. The curse placed upon the Greek God of Gravity had been lifted. And she had never been happier.

25

Roomies

To keep standing water at a minimum, Archibald showered in the mornings and Brock showered at night. While the tub usually drained in the meantime, each room-mate agreed to preventative measures to avoid overflow. In practice, that meant bailing a few buckets of water into the sink after every shower with the bathroom garbage pail.

This morning, before Archibald could bail his first bucket, a slab of drywall fell from the ceiling around the ventilation fan and splashed into the tub. Archibald had seen signs of such decay for months. Cracks, drywall bubbles, and the occasional powdery dusting when the upstairs tenants walked around too fast were normal occurrences. But this was the first time any of those blisters had actually popped. While he fished out the fallen slabs from the tub, Archibald wondered how long until the whole ceiling caved in. Days? Weeks? Months?

It turned out to be a matter of hours.

When the bathroom ceiling popped later that afternoon, it covered the tub in a moldy borscht, equal parts pink insulation, white sheetrock, and brown wood rot. Brock saw the damage first. Yet when he did, he was already late for work, so rather than remove the debris, he washed himself around and amongst it, all the while muttering cusswords about how Archibald was somehow to blame.

Speak of the devil.

A knock at the door. "Hey, man, you mind if I use the toilet quick before I head to Jerry's?" Archibald said through the door. Jerry, a decent friend and a good drug-dealer, lived in the apartment complex across the street.

"For what?" Brock said as he took his foot out of the tub, placed it onto the tile floor, and reached for the doorknob.

Archibald's answer made him recoil.

"Do that at Jerry's," Brock said.

Without another word, Archibald stormed across the hallway and exited the apartment. In a moment, when all was silent but the ambient noise of water falling from the showerhead, Brock raised his foot from the bathroom floor and lowered it back into the filthy tub water. Before it reached the slimy acrylic bottom, a drywall screw punctured his plantar fascia, causing him to lose balance and fall.

Archibald returned from Jerry's a few hours later. His sneakers squished as soon as he walked past the welcome mat in the dark kitchen. Reading the direction of the water, he tracked the wetness into the hallway. There he saw puddles—puddles illuminated by the lone light in the apartment creeping out from underneath the bathroom door.

Inside, the shower was still running.

26

Reverse Robin Hood

S ifting through garbage for five cent-cans is the lowest form of work in our society. So low that despite the labor, it isn't even considered work. It's a hobby for the homeless, the poor, and the mentally ill.

Strange; to me, mentally ill are people who literally throw out money with every meal.

My inner capitalist saw an opportunity in this dichotomy. It awaited in the trash—so I dove in, business casual attire on and all. My seemingly inappropriate dress had a purpose. I sought to win over onlookers, change the culture of the 'act.' I wanted them to see my clothes as a type of uniform, and to see my efforts for what they really were: an entrepreneurial venture, not some act of desperation.

Opinions differed on my actions. Some deemed my actions despicable, even thievish. To them, I was a sort of reverse Robin Hood, a man who stole from the poor and gave to himself.

Others applauded my entrepreneurial spirit. True supporters

donated their cans for free. The business savvy entered into fee splitting agreements with me on obtained profits from their personal can stash. The neat freaks paid me to take all cans off their hands if I could get it done faster than the sanitation department. The more I honed my craft, the more I got support. And consequently, the more fellow can collectors suffered.

That got me a visit from Alnaz.

"Steer clear of their cans," he said, in less than friendly words.

Heeding that warning, I passed up my normal walk home through back alleys for the subway. At least for now, the empty happy hour bottles fresh off the bar, ripe for picking, had to wait. The old way wasn't safe anymore.

The subway doors opened at my stop. I followed the track of solidified gum spats up the stairs of my local station, Alnaz's words of caution on repeat in my mind. The first thing I saw when I reached the top step was the unfamiliar face of a home-less man begging for change. Considering I knew the 'locals' who used this corner, I found that strange. Yet by the looks of him, he wasn't new to the streets. Nor was his face, so shrunken and shriveled that it was turning into jam, by any means forgettable.

It also seemed to limit his vision. At least that's what I figured when I saw that the empty Pepsi can between his left foot and the curb was still unclaimed. Too feeble to fear, I couldn't resist, I lunged at the prize between his legs. Before he could counter my encroachment, the can was mine.

Aware that homeless folk are skilled in the rhetorical arts, I anticipated a snappy insult from my adversary that a passerby would outwardly ignore but inwardly find funny. This time, however, none came. All I heard from the mouth of the shrunken head was heavy breathing, then coughing, then the sound of blood spatter on the sidewalk.

His sorry state hit the sensitive notes of my conscience, causing me to hand over my five-cent prize.

At first, he smiled a bloody smile and welcomed my offering. Then he scanned my face, noticed my business casual dress, and pulled back. He knew who I was. No real surprise there. When Alnaz spoke, word got round faster than the subways.

"Keep it," he said with a sly teethy grin outlined in blood. "You're gunna need it more than me."

27

Campsite Post 42

Cowboy slot machines at Indian casinos are rigged. I wish I knew that earlier. It would have saved me a night of sleeping in my car.

Campsite forty-two was available for the evening. No wonder. In a park filled with souped-up RVs, a spot without electrical hookups was no spot at all. The days of roughing it on vacation, I suppose, were over. Even in the middle of the woods, I'd be the only one around without air conditioning.

There were benefits to my sorry state. No concern for electricity meant I could choose a spot purely on curb appeal. With its striking views of the sun setting over the plains, Campsite forty-two was a no-brainer. So was getting firewood before dark.

First, though, I needed to register.

I exited the car and walked down Campsite forty-two's tiny gravel driveway to the post with its namesake, positioned just off the road. Pinned to the post was a yellow envelope containing a document for campers to fill out and leave money —$20 per night. Fair enough. I grabbed a pen and input the required info. When I searched my wallet to pay the fee, all I had were two fifties.

Struggling to part from either bill easily, I searched for defects to justify a sacrifice. The task proved easier than expected. One fifty-dollar bill had blue-ink scribbled on President Grant's bowtie. That one went in the envelope. Outside the envelope I wrote "NEED CHANGE!" in big bold font.

Then I pinned my payment to Campsite post forty-two and went to gather firewood.

For a campsite with so many occupied spots, it sure was silent. The yells and screams and roars of laughter of children are the chorus of campgrounds. Tonight though, nothing. Where were they? Their parents? Anyone else? Every outdoor chair was empty, yet smoke still rose from charcoal grills, riderless bicycles were frozen in postures that looked odd without a person nearby.

By the time my teepee fire munched its first course of kindling, hail started to fall. I knew it was hail because of the pounding it gave my windshield. *Jesus, don't break the windshield,* I thought as I ran for the car, hoping to muffle the sinister shouts of the banshee wind.

Lightning flashed over the plains. An ominous vortex of terror spun in my direction. The friends of the banshee wind had answered her call.

A few swipes at my iPhone informed me to seek refuge within the cement walls of the campground restroom. I wasn't alone when I got there.

"Just made it," a voice said from inside the shower stall. I had just finished a mad dash across the campsite, so I was stooped over, sucking wind. This put me at eye-level with the waist of the speaker, which also put me at eye-level with his ridiculous cowboy revolver. Other waists were nearby. Those waists also had guns, albeit less ridiculous ones.

I had found the campers. And I had found their guns.

Fucking open carry laws.

"Not many tornadoes where I'm from," I said, panting, trying hard to force friendliness.

"Where's that?" the man with the ridiculous cowboy revolver asked.

"The City," I said. Their silent response indicated they found me arrogant for calling my city, "The City." To soften the mood, I added, "I'm a little out of my element."

"Maybe out there, but not in here. Doesn't New York love the idea of men, women and children sharing bathrooms? The way I see it, you should feel right at home," the man with the ridiculous cowboy revolver said. Based on the number of laughs his statement received, I underestimated the number of campers stuck in the restroom.

"What brings you down here?" the man with the ridiculous cowboy revolver asked.

"Heading west. Just passing through. Road trip," I said.

Someone creaked open the door to peek outside. The banshee wind headed back to hell. Calm night returned to take its place.

"They come and go fast here. But we're good now. Enjoy your evening, Yank," the man with the ridiculous cowboy revolver said as he put out his hand. "Name's Nathaniel Davis."

"Parker Welsh," I said, extending my hand.

I felt the after-effects of his python grip the whole walk back to Campsite forty-two. The pain lessened when I saw that my car survived. The worst of the storm must have hit elsewhere. Morning, I suppose, would tell all, at least that's what I convinced myself of as I reclined in my driver's seat and began to nod off.

A pickup truck pulled up to my site and flashed its lights. Nathaniel Davis got out. "Campground collecting payment. Oh hello, Mr. Welsh," he said.

"It's pinned to the post," I said, growing nervous.

Nathaniel Davis walked over to the Campsite forty-two post. Every few steps along the way, he adjusted his belt buckle to compensate for the weight of his ridiculous cowboy revolver.

"Not here," he said.

I went to check. Nathaniel Davis was right.

"It was here. The envelope with the money must have blown away in the storm," I said.

He shook his head with disdain. "Never heard that one before."

I couldn't resist. "I don't owe the campground. They owe me —$30 to be exact."

"Sorry, son. No handouts in Oklahoma. You'll have to go back to New York for that," Nathaniel Davis said.

I paid the fucker the fifty-dollar bill still in my wallet so he'd get the hell away from me. He immediately handed back the right change.

"You sleeping in a tent?" he asked, beginning to fill out the same type of yellow envelope as I did earlier.

"Does that matter?" I asked.

"It might," he said.

"No tent. Just the car," I said.

"All right then. You know your right rear tire is cracked. Needs fixing soon or the rubber will expand, and the tires will blow, especially if you're going long distance. Don't want to get caught out here without a vehicle."

I didn't like the smile that came with the comment.

"You have a spare?" he asked.

"Nope," I said.

He shook his head how my grandfather did whenever I operated some obscure woodworking tool with futility.

Once Nathaniel Davis left, I went back in my car, only to be tortured by bad dreams involving tornadoes and slot machines and men with ridiculous cowboy revolvers. Morning couldn't come soon enough. I woke at first light, when there was just enough visibility to notice the new tire leaning against Camp-site post forty-two.

Above the tire, tacked against the post, was a muddy yellow envelope with the word "NEED CHANGE" written across the front. Underneath the "Need Change" phrase was another phrase, written even more conspicuously in red: "REFUND."

Folded inside the envelope was a fifty-dollar bill with President Grant's bow tie colored in blue.

28

Dearest Q

"Nineteen..." Dev said as his chin struggled to rise above the pullup bar.

One more rep, and he'd reach twenty, a personal best. A breath to calm his vascular system, and then another to cool his red face, then up his dangling pronated arms went for one final push.

Goal achieved.

Celebration ensued. An excited Dev jumped off the bar and threw a flurry of shadow punches at the bookstacks crowding his hallway. When he finished throwing haymakers, he paraded past the gliding glass doors and onto the balcony, fancying the metal bannister outside was a turnbuckle and he was a champion and the night sky was a packed arena with flashing lights rather than a second-story panorama of a deteriorated parking lot dressed in dirty snow.

On a warmer night without icy bannisters Dev would scale the top rail and balance on the end post to really sell the fantasy. Lucky for him, sub-zero temperatures prevented such escapades—otherwise the projectile that just fell past his face would have turned his head to mush. Down below, the smoking snowhole the projectile created stirred his curiosity, compelling him to investigate.

The bin lodged in the snowdrift smoked from the ashes of handwritten letters. Dev fanned the flames of a survivor and skimmed its contents. Once he finished, he stood, dumbfounded. The ashen paper he beheld was a jewel in a crown of fire. Were there others? The question obligated him to rescue all that were salvageable. By the end of his efforts, fifty letters, all sent by "Anonymous," all addressed to a "Dearest Q," were saved.

He began to read them, and fast confirmed his intuition. The first letter was no anomaly. All of them were fire jewels. All of them deserved a spot on his makeshift library upstairs, side by side with the other masters. But where? The letters, composed over a few months, had no author. Dev decided he'd stash them in the Q section. First, though, he had to read them, and continue reading them—up the stairs, in the bathroom, at dinner, during tv time—to completion.

Or until a knock sounded at the door.

"Good evening, I believe you have some letters," the man standing on the welcome mat said. Dev knew his face from occasionally crossing paths in the lobby.

"Just a second," Dev said.

When he returned with the stack of letters, the man in the hallway was flicking his cigarette lighter with a look of resolution.

"Why burn something so beautiful?" Dev asked the man.

Inwardly, he asked himself a different question: whether he owed it to society to prevent their destruction.

"Q is my wife. But I am not the writer," the man said.

29

The Desecration of the Chesterfield Sofa

A trail of clothes led from the secretary's desk to Dustin's office.

"How professional," Tiff said to her husband as Alice crawled out from under his legs

"I don't like her," Tiff said. "Get rid of her."

"Why's that?" Dustin asked, buttoning up his shirt.

"Too pretty. I'd rather your secretary's look more like Ornella," Tiff said.

"Ornella before or after you ran a chainsaw through her chest?" Dustin asked.

"She had it coming," Tiff said. "Now get rid of Alice before she suffers the same fate."

"If you insist," Dustin said, trying to hide his unhappiness at the request.

Sensing his disappointment, Tiff advanced her case. "C'mon, she isn't even good at her job. She answers phones worse than Amber."

"How many times did you hear Amber answer the phone?"

Dustin asked.

Tiff bit her bottom lip. "Enough where I wanted to staple her lips together."

"You came pretty close," Dustin said, remembering how Tiff had drilled Amber's mouth shut.

"Alice is the best notetaker I've ever had. She gets down every word of my meetings. Better recall than Brad, too," Dustin said.

"Bringing up the Brad days is never a winning argument for you, Dust. Get rid of her tonight, or I will, that's the end of it," Tiff said as she walked past Alice's desk and then the adjacent chesterfield sofa. With disgust, her fingers slid across the back covers of the brown leather, searching for clues that she already had the answer for. Shame what the classic piece of furniture she custom-built for her husband's waiting room had become.

It was a relief when her fingers reached the end of the sofa and continued onto the basement stairs handrail. A slight slicing sensation from a splinter ended such relief. Further investigation of her finger proved the wood escaped unpunished, leaving just a tiny, barely bleeding, cut behind. The splinter's escape, combined with her aggravation over the fate of the chesterfield sofa, made Tiff search for a proper place to direct her anger. A lightbulb flashed in her mind right when a lightbulb turned on behind the basement door. She had her scapegoat.

"Also, it's been months since your downstairs tenants paid rent," Tiff yelled down the hall.

"I'll take care of it," Dustin said, looking at his polka-dotted lanyard coiled on the corner of his desk that held his spare key to the downstairs apartment.

"Remember, take care of getting rid of her too," Tiff said, sneering at Alice. "I'm serious."

Initially, Dustin planned to honor his wife's instructions, he really did. The closer the plan came to action though, the harder it was to part with Alice. Her big round eyes got all watery the second he did. And then she started to sniffle. No secretary before Alice had been so emotionally attached.

Soon, they were back on the chesterfield sofa.

In the middle of their now naked embrace, the front door beeped four times. When those four beeps undid the deadlock, there was no question who was inside the office. Before the lovers could cover up, Tiff entered the hallway dragging an ax. For a moment, Dustin wondered whether his tiny wife had the strength to wield it. When the blade split Alice's face in two, he had his answer.

Rather than dislodge the weapon from her victim's neck, Tiff mounted her already unclothed husband, leaving the secretary to smoke and spark on the floor.

"You think she'll sell without a head?" Tiff asked Dustin when they were done.

"Only if they can install a new one. It's her best feature. People go to town on those mouths," Dustin said, wiping sweat from his brow.

"Who are you going to hire now?" Tiff asked, burrowing deeper into her husband's arms.

"Maybe Ornella?" Dustin said. "It's convenient."

Tiff laughed at the absurdity of the statement. Ornella was all spare parts by now... or so she thought.

When she turned to the wall beside the basement staircase and beheld a reconstructed Ornella, still adorning her massive shoulder-to-belly chainsaw scar, but newly equipped with a new pair of gigantic tits that clashed with her skin color, Tiff knew she had been mistaken.

She didn't even bother to look at her husband. Tiff was too

disgusted with his lies and too fixed on reopening the scar she'd created on Ornella's mended midsection. Tiff was tough. But Ornella was a more quarrelsome program than Alice, and had better memory. Struggle ensued.

At first, Tiff subdued her attacker. Then a hand ripped a clump of hair from her head. A hand, Tiff quickly realized, that couldn't be Ornella's, since they were grappling.

Dustin? Nope. Dustin was cowering in the corner. He couldn't even help himself.

The hand full of hair belonged to another woman, a woman with screw holes punctured deep into each side of her face so she looked like a colander... Amber.

"Dust! I can't handle them both!" Tiff yelled.

As she said this, another large pair of arms wrapped around her legs and hoisted her into the air. There he was, a new and improved Brad, hardly recognizable from when Tiff gave him a gasoline shower in the snow and dried him off with a blowtorch.

Tiff tried to undo Brad's grip. She made her upper-body vulnerable to Amber and Ornella in the process. Both seized on the opportunity to latch on to one arm each. Now with Brad at the helm, the three assailants lifted Tiff above their heads and paraded her down the basement stairs.

Dustin, nonexistent until now, waited for them on the bottom step. Across from him, the door to the basement apartment cracked open. The polka-dotted key lanyard dangled from the doorknob.

"You never threw them out?" a defeated and captive Tiff said while passing her husband.

"I bought great policies to protect against wife damage," he said. Then he closed the door behind them with his foot.

30

The Painting

The hallways of their home had more trees than their backyard. Alfonso's mother was responsible for that. Ever since they moved to the city, she'd committed to landscape painting. The hobby relaxed her, and more importantly, helped her cope with a chronic longing for the countryside of her youth.

Given her large body of work, specific paintings faded from memory, disappearing along with the frequent changes to the apartment's interior design—with one exception. The painting opposite her bed survived stylistic transitions that nothing else could because of its taste and utility. In other words, the painting had purpose. That purpose was to serve as his mother's artificial window to wake up to every morning. By seeing it first thing, the painting elevated her mood and counterbalanced the depression that came with turning around and facing the yelling, screaming, honking horns, bicycle bells, policeman whistles, and other generalized chaos concocted by the chaos of the city below.

Alphonso hadn't seen the painting opposite his mother's bed in some time. But that didn't matter. The important images of life never leave the gallery of the mind. The painting had been exhibited in Alphonso's mind since preschool. It reached featured exhibit status shortly thereafter. Back then, they'd sit on mom's bed and smile in silence at the world occurring inside the frame. Eventually the thoughts generating those smiles turned to words. They'd talk about the white cottage with the thatched roof where the birds belted out songs and built nests. They'd assess the wildflower blooms; the fruit growth on the apple trees; the health of the slender birch trees overhanging the tiny suspension bridge that separated the cottage from the road, where brook trout lurked in the shadows, stalking flies. The conversation wouldn't end until they settled on which of the background mountains they'd climb today in their dreams.

In middle school, Alfonso had become increasingly aware of the sacrifices his mother made for them to stay in the city. From then on, he vowed to make something of himself. And once he did, he'd buy his mother the real version of the country cottage in her painting.

Efforts to achieve this goal started small. Still too young to work, Alphonso searched for change wherever he could find it —on the street, in couches, in vending machines, on laundromat floors, in cans that he could exchange for cash at the supermarket. Such search and salvage practices never went away, but they left center stage for more profitable tasks. Once he reached working age, he had jobs, (often times two) which proved more profitable. That was the story through high school, college, and med-school, at least before residency.

After residency, the real money started to flow. At thirty-five he started house hunting. By forty-two he pulled the trigger on a place.

A year of renovations later, to the house and the surrounding landscape, the property was identical to the cottage painting. Thus, it was finally time to invite his mother, entirely unaware of everything— from the middle-school pact to make something of himself to the real estate purchase thirty years later— to see it for the first time.

Per usual, his mother was waiting for him on the sidewalk when he pulled up.

"Where we going?" she asked.

"It's a surprise," Alfonso said, helping her into the car.

She fell asleep as soon as her bum hit the seat. Nothing new there. For as long as Alfonso could remember, his mother's eyes shut the second she felt wheels underfoot. The near-automatic response developed from a combination of overwork and a lifetime spent on public transportation.

"Wake up, ma, I want to show you something," Alfonso said as he turned down the road where the property was located. There it was, their first full view of the cottage.

When Alphonso heard silence, he turned to his mother to see what was wrong. The massive smile spread across her face eased his anxieties. As it had with the painting itself, silence equated to elation.

"It's yours, mom. I bought it for you," Alphonso said.

She kissed him on the cheek. "Tell me what it looks like," she said.

"Why?" I asked.

"I've gone blind since you last saw me. It's been a while," she said.

"But you smiled when we turned down the road," Alphonso said.

She smiled again. Then she said, "When you gotta go you gotta go."

31

The Eyoyluoefazlopian Accord

An emaciated old woman with a nest of coily black hair stood at the lectern in the dimly lit basement conference room. The table next to her held a stack of papers. The administrator at the door, Cynthia, according to the Mammoth Cave National Park ID, told Richter to grab a copy and sit.

The paper, lettered in skillful calligraphy, was a one-page document titled "the Eyoyluoefazlopian Accord."

Seriously? Richter became a park ranger for the fieldwork and to avoid reading big words fancily dressed. Eyoyluoefazlopian? On his first day of work? Really?

Before he could continue worrying, the old woman at the lectern spoke:

"My name is Eyoyluoefazlop. I am an American Vampire. No, I am not the type of vampire you know from folklore. The ones with the affinity for castles and everything else gothic, those are our uppity European cousins. By the end of my talk today, you'll appreciate the distinction.

"To begin, American Vampires are forest folk, lovers of the

wood, cave-dwellers. We are also matriarchal, which is why, at least in my view, we remain, and our European brethren do not. For how long though... who knows. Our population is conservation dependent. Besides the recluses, we live in one general location—that location is beneath your feet.

"Your confused stares are understandable. Allow me to better articulate...

"Mammoth Cave National Park is a front. Its 400-mile cave system, the largest in the world, is an American Vampire sanctuary. This is how it happened:

"In 1609 I witnessed what historians now call the Beaver Wars, one of the first conflicts between European settlers and Native Americans. Before the Beaver Wars, the industrialized death associated with gunfire was foreign to me. In so much wasteful death and destruction, I saw an opportunity to flatten my fangs. Rather than hunt, a task that all American vampires despise, I would scavenge. I would feed off the wasted dead of human war.

"My vow—never kill— fast attracted other American vampires. Before long, a whole band of us were scavenging skirmish sites, then battles, then entire wars. At this point, I can say with confidence that an American Vampire has 'dined' at every sizeable military confrontation in North American History.

"Understand that all this was a means to an end. I had no intentions of scavenging forever, not unless you think the buffet prepared for you upstairs makes you a scavenger. My intentions were to bide my time, wait for the right opportunity to make a deal.

"In 1812 I got that opportunity. America had just declared war against the United Kingdom. This presented a problem. Due to British naval blockades, Americans could not import gunpowder. I was in Kentucky at the time when I heard the solution.

"'Mine Mammoth Cave for potassium chloride. Then ship it back east to the factories where it can mix with charcoal and sulfur and turn into gunpowder.' From the mouths of four drunken white guys at a bar in 1812 to your ears.

"The way history is told today, with the help of 70 of their slaves, these white men mined Mammoth Cave and made monumental contributions to the war effort. Further questioning renders that absurd. How did so few men, inexperienced in mining and devoid of any substantive knowledge of the massive Mammoth Cave system, pull this off... from extraction to shipment?

"They didn't.

"I did.

"Shortly after hearing the four drunks discuss the matter, I penned a letter to then-President James Madison, explaining the strength of the idea and the unachievable task of mere men in carrying it out. The job called for vampires.

"Madison was too smart to disagree. In his letter to me, the original of which is now buried in top-secret files at the National Archives, the President said that he dealt with the four drunks, meaning he paid them off, and the job was mine.

"These were the terms of the secret deal:

"Madison would give the American Vampire Mammoth Cave and agree to feed us there in perpetuity. In exchange for that, the American Vampire would supply all the potassium chloride needed for the war effort. And given our strength, our speed, and yes, our ability to fly, we would rapidly transport it back east to the chemical plants for manufacture.

"The American Vampires has been here ever since, first under the guise of fake property records, and then inside

Mammoth Cave National Park, a front for our sanctuary. We still receive blood from the American government, a process that has thankfully advanced since the pre-refrigeration days. Back then, our blood came coagulated. To feed, we needed to mix it with water and eat it like paste. Now, with refrigeration (who do you think came up with that) and advancements in transfusions (who do you think came up with that) we have our own blood bank right here at Mammoth cave. Therefore, we drink our blood cool and fresh, always from a fancy glass, always with a straw. The deal looks a lot better now. Except for this last part.

"Each year, the government asks me to welcome you, the new Mammoth Cave Ranger staff, to the national park and share this story. Call me a conservative, a title I've earned since I'm 6000 years old, but the Parks Department could save the money earmarked for my expensive speaking fees and just give you a copy of the sheet in front of you—the Eyoyluoefazlopian Accord. I wouldn't go as far as to say that this document is a symbol of American Human/American Vampire friendship, but it keeps both sides civil... for the most part.

"In closing, good luck in your service to Mammoth Cave National Park. I assure every Ranger of civility when they enter Eyoy on their daily beat. Don't look so scared. It may sound strange now, but many of you will find love down there and decide to stay, sometimes forever. Trust me, the slow aging process of a spouse helps a lot more than couple's therapy. Plus, a federal government pension goes a long way over the course of a few thousand years. But I'm not here to give financial advice. I'll save that for the Wall Street Execs flying in next week for a 'tour.'

"For now, I'll just say thank you for listening and open the floor for questions."

www.ingramcontent.com/pod-product-compliance
Lightning Source LLC
Chambersburg PA
CBHW071008120726
47910CB00004B/1429